PART ONE

3

HEY LOOK! AN AFRICAN DANCE WORKSHOP! LET'S GO!!

WHAT?!

WHAT MAKES YOU THINK I'M INTERESTED IN AFRICAN DANCE?! DON'T YOU EVEN KNOW ME BY NOW? I DON'T DANCE!!

YOU NEVER WANNA TRY ANYTHING NEW! YOU'RE JUST LIKE AN OLD MAN! YOU'RE AFRAID TO HAVE FUN!

LOOK, IF THIS IS YOUR IDEA OF FUN -- THEN GO! DON'T LET ME STOP YOU!

I WANT TO SHARE THE EXPERIENCE WITH YOU STUPID! THAT'S THE FUN!

YOU DON'T KNOW ANYTHING ABOUT BEING IN A RELATIONSHIP! IT TAKES WORK! SOMETIMES YOU'VE GOTTA COMPROMISE!

WHY SHOULD I? I NEVER ASK OR EXPECT ANYTHING FROM YOU.

BAH.

THE FOLLOWING DAY...

HI SETH--IT'S JUST ME MAKING MY DAILY CALL. YEAH-- HAHA! SO WHAT'S NEW? WHAT? YOU FOUND SOME OLD VIEW-MASTER REELS! REALLY? HOW MANY? WOW! HOLD ON, LET ME GO GET MY "WANT" LIST...

AN HOUR LATER..

--WELL MY FAVORITE PEANUTS STRIPS ARE THE EARLY ONES-- BEFORE SNOOPY STARTED WALKING AROUND ON HIS HIND LEGS. RIGHT. HEY! SPEAKING OF LEGS, REMEMBER THE STRIP WHERE CHARLIE BROWN-- YEAH! THAT'S THE ONE! HAHAHA

LATER STILL..

--OR HOW ABOUT THAT LINE IN MANHATTAN WHEN WOODY'S IN THE CAB AND SAYS, "YOU LOOK SO BEAUTIFUL I CAN HARDLY KEEP MY EYES ON THE METER." HAHAHA! ANYWAY-- BLAH BLAH BLAH BLAH...

SLAM!

UH-OH! TRISH IS HOME -- I'D BETTER GET OFF THE PHONE! TALK TO YOU LATER SETH -- 'BYE.

YOU DON'T HAVE TO GET OFF THE PHONE JUST CUZ I'M HOME!

I KNOW BUT I NEED SOLITUDE WHEN I'M ON THE PHONE OTHERWISE I FEEL INHIBITED.

WELL EXCUUUSE ME!

ANYWAY, I'M STARVING! WHY DON'T YOU COME IN HERE AND HAVE DINNER WITH ME? I'VE BEEN DYING TO TELL YOU ABOUT MY DAY. YOU WOULDN'T BELIEVE WHAT HAPPENED. FIRST I WENT TO...

I ALREADY ATE. BESIDES, I'M ALL TALKED OUT-- I JUST WANNA READ NOW.

9

MORNING..

Z

'BYE LUV-- I'M GOING TO WORK NOW. SEE YOU TONIGHT.

BLEH! COFFEE-BREATH! GET AWAY!!

YOU ASSHOLE! I'M TRYING TO BE NICE BUT ALL YOU EVER DO IS CRITICIZE ME! LOOK AT YOU-- YOUR BREATH STINKS WORSE THAN MINE! YOU LOOK LIKE A BUM!!

GROAN
THERE YOU GO AGAIN...

SLAM!

BAH! WHO NEEDS HER?

LET'S SEE NOW-- WHAT CAN I USE? MAYBE AN OLD PORN FILM? NAH, I'M TIRED OF USING THOSE SAME OLD SCENES --- MAYBE THAT GIRL I SAW IN THE LIBRARY YESTERDAY -- NAH, TOO MILKFED. AAHH-- I HAVE IT...

HI THERE. NEED ANY HELP?

FRANKIE! W-WHAT ARE YOU DOING HERE?!

20

23

HI POOPIE!

YAAH!

QUIT SNEAKIN' UP ON ME!! YOU KNOW I'M TICKLISH!! NOW STOP DOING IT!!!

CHILL OUT.

TWO HOURS LATER..

BLAH BLAH BLAH BLAH BLAH BLAH BLAH BLAH BLAH

I CAN'T STOP STARING AT HER! SUCH BEAUTY. ⸮SIGH⸮

HEY JOE -- YOU'VE BEEN AWFULLY QUIET TONIGHT.

HAVE I? WELL I GUESS I JUST DON'T HAVE MUCH TO SAY FOR A CHANGE. HEH...HEH.. HEH...

HEY BABY -- WHY DON'T YOU SHOW SETH THOSE VIEW-MASTER REELS YOU BROUGHT?

OH--YEAH! WAIT'LL YOU SEE THESE -- YOU'RE GONNA LOVE 'EM!

Y-YOU GOT MORE VIEW-MASTER REELS? WHICH ONES? DO I NEED THEM? WHERE DID YOU FIND THEM?

WOW! THESE ARE GREAT! I NEVER KNEW THERE WAS A BIBLE SERIES.

TRISH GOT THEM FOR ME. I ALSO HAVE CHARLIE BROWN, THE FLINTSTONES AND SOME REALLY OLD FAIRY TALES.

LET US SEE! LET US SEE!

CLICK CLICK

HERE FRANKIE! TAKE A LOOK! GO AHEAD! YOU'LL LOVE THESE -- I PROMISE!

THAT'S OKAY. GIVE IT TO SOMEONE ELSE -- I'M REALLY NOT INTERESTED.

ZIP!

NONSENSE! C'MON! JUST TAKE A LOOK! TRUST ME! JUST ONE LOOK! C'MON! DON'T BE AFRAID! C'MON!

NO THANK YOU. I SAID I'M NOT INTERESTED.

SHOVE SHOVE

ANYWAY, AS I WAS SAYING -- I'D REALLY LIKE TO GET A TATTOO SOON. NOTHING FANCY Y'KNOW, JUST--

B-BUT THESE'RE THE OLD PUPPET KIND. THEY'RE LIKE MINIATURE.. UH.. UM..

BAH!

THAT NIGHT..

I GOT THE FEELING FRANKIE DIDN'T LIKE ME TOO MUCH. WHAT DO YOU THINK?

SHE PROBABLY DOESN'T. LAST WEEK WHEN I MENTIONED THAT PORN VIDEO YOU RENTED SHE GOT REAL DISGUSTED AND--

WHAT?! YOU TOLD HER?!

YEAH, WHAT DO YOU CARE? YOU'RE THE ONE WHO KEEPS SAYING THAT THERE'S NOTHING WRONG WITH PORNOGRAPHY. HELL, YOU KEEP MENTIONING IT IN YOUR DAMN COMICS ANYWAY.

PART
TWO

-- DID YOU KNOW THAT THERE ARE OVER FIVE MILLION BLAH BLAH BLAH BLAH BLAH BLAH

WOW, REALLY? HMMMMMM.. INTERESTING..

UH--EXCUSE ME. I'VE GOTTA GO TO THE BATHROOM.

CERTAINLY.

HEY JOE--HAVE SOME BACON! I'VE GOT TWO WHOLE POUNDS OF IT HERE.

UH--NO THANKS. I'VE HEARD THAT THE SODIUM NITRATE IN IT CAN CAUSE CANCER.

THAT'S RIDICULOUS! SODIUM NITRATE'S JUST A NECESSARY SALT USED IN THE CURING OF MEAT. I BELIEVE IT COMES FROM CHILE. AND MEAT'S AN IMPORTANT SOURCE OF PROTEIN AND ESSENTIAL FATTY ACIDS. LOOK IT UP IF YOU DON'T BELIEVE ME. WHY, FROM THE DAWN OF TIME, MAN HAS BEEN CARNIVOROUS AND--

OH REALLY? UH-HUH..HMM..

RRRRRING!

TELEPHONE! I'LL GET IT IN MY ROOM!

OOPS--BACON'S BURNING!

36

HEH--HEH--LOOKS LIKE OL' C.W. IS RUNNING OUT OF **FOOD**. PRETTY SOON HE'S EITHER GONNA HAVE TO GET A JOB OR GO ON A DIET.

HMMM--I COULD HAVE SWORN I HAD MORE MILK THAN THIS. I'LL BET C.W.'s BEEN SWIPING IT. I SHOULD MARK THE LEVEL AND TRAP HIM.

HI JOE. LOOK AT ALL THE GROCERIES THEY GAVE ME DOWN AT THE **FOOD BANK!** SARDINES, BEANS AND ALL SORTS OF CANNED GOODS! YOU'RE WELCOME TO HAVE SOME.

THAT'S OKAY CHARLES.

BAH! WHAT A **LEECH** ON SOCIETY! WHAT KIND OF WORLD ARE WE LIVING IN THAT WON'T LET **DEADBEATS** STARVE?

THAT WEEKEND..

UH--Y'GONNA EAT THAT LETTUCE, TOMATO AND ONION?

NOPE. HELP YOURSELF.

OBOY! IT'S LIKE A LITTLE SALAD!

CRUNCH CRUNCH Y'KNOW, IF I WAS STILL LIVING WITH TRISH, I COULDN'T EAT THIS RAW ONION. SHE HATED ONION-BREATH.

SPEAKING OF TRISH--

40

41

OH GOD--LOOK AT THAT ORIENTAL GIRL OVER AT THE NEXT TABLE! **SHE'S GORGEOUS!** ≷ WHIMPER ≷ GOD IT HURTS-- I CAN'T TAKE IT..

YOU POOR BASTARD. YOU REALLY SUFFER, DON'T YOU?

TELL ME ABOUT IT. I'VE BEEN LIKE THIS EVER SINCE I HIT PUBERTY. IT'S AWFUL. SOME GIRLS ARE JUST SO BEAUTIFUL AND I WANT SO BADLY JUST TO TOUCH THEM AND--AND--

WELL I GOT NEWS FOR YOU PAL--

--THESE SUPER-SKINNY, MODEL-TYPE GIRLS YOU'RE ALWAYS DROOLING OVER ARE **WAY** OUT OF YOUR LEAGUE! THEY WANT POWERFUL, CONFIDENT, MODEL-TYPE GUYS-- NOT CHEAP, LITTLE, WHINING NEUROTICS LIKE YOU! SO QUIT TORTURING YOURSELF.

I KNOW--YOU'RE RIGHT.

BESIDES, YOU'VE GOT TRISH. WHY CAN'T YOU JUST BE SATISFIED WITH HER?

SHE'S THE ONE WHO'S NOT SATISFIED WITH ME! SHE KEEPS TRYING TO CHANGE ME AND I REFUSE TO! THAT'S WHY SHE'S TOO MAD TO EVEN VISIT ME THIS WEEKEND!

THAT'S BULLSHIT. SHE'S TOLD ME HOW YOU'RE ALWAYS TELLING HER SHE'S FAT AND--

I NEVER SAID SHE WAS FAT! SHE'S THE ONE THAT'S ALWAYS SAYING SHE'S FAT! I JUST GET SO SICK OF HEARING IT THAT SOMETIMES I AGREE! THAT'S ALL!

SHE SAID YOU EVEN CALL HER "FROG-BODY".

"FROG-BODY" WAS **HER** IDEA! SHE STARTED IT! I JUST THOUGHT IT WAS FUNNY AND USED IT LIKE A NICKNAME! IT WAS A TERM OF ENDEARMENT!

REAL ENDEARING JOE.

BAH. LET'S CHANGE THE SUBJECT.

OKAY. HOW'S C.W.?

CHRIST, DON'T EVEN ASK. EVERY DAY I HAVE TO LISTEN TO HIM RIGHT OUTSIDE MY DOOR-- GRUNTING AND BURPING WHILE EATING POUNDS OF BACON. PLUS NOW HE BRINGS HIS RADIO WITH HIM AND BLARES ALL SORTS OF TALK PROGRAMS AND SHITTY MUSIC AND--AND-- AAAUUGH! I CAN'T TAKE IT ANYMORE I TELLYA!

CAN'T YOU HAVE A TALK WITH HIM?

TALK WITH HIM?! THAT'S THE LAST THING I WANNA DO! HE'S A WINDBAG! I PRACTICALLY NEVER EVEN LEAVE MY ROOM FOR FEAR I'LL GET STUCK LISTENING TO HIS RAMBLING!

CAN'T YOU JUST TURN UP YOUR OWN RADIO SO YOU WON'T HEAR HIM ANYMORE?

I NEED COMPLETE SILENCE WHEN I'M WORKING.

THEN STAY UP LATE AND WORK WHILE HE'S SLEEPING.

I CAN'T. HE KEEPS TOTALLY ERRATIC HOURS. HE'S OFTEN UP ALL NIGHT.

THEN GET A PAIR OF EARPLUGS.

BUT EARPLUGS COST MONEY.

WHOOOOA! I'M ON THE TREADMILL! WHOOOA!

VERY FUNNY.

AAAHH-- RELAX.

44

PORTFOLIO? OH, YOU'RE A PHOTOGRAPHER, HUH? HMMM--INTERESTING...

HERE'S A JOB I SHOT LAST YEAR THAT I STILL HAVEN'T BEEN PAID FOR.

THAT REMINDS ME OF A SUPERHERO COMIC I COLORED TWO YEARS AGO THAT *I'M* STILL WAITING TO GET PAID FOR! THOSE BASTARDS OWE ME THOUSANDS AND I'M NOT PROSTITUTING MYSELF LIKE THAT AGAIN UNTIL I GET PAID.

C'MON, EVERYONE GETS SCREWED AT LEAST ONCE. DON'T LET THAT STOP YOU.

LISTEN-- IF SUPERHERO COMICS IS WHERE THE MONEY IS, THEN GO FOR IT. THE STARVING ARTIST ROUTINE IS FOR THE BIRDS. Y'GOTTA MAKE HAY WHILE THE SUN IS SHINING. Y'FOLLOW ME?

FORGET IT. I'D RATHER STARVE. ONCE Y'GET USED TO MAKING MONEY, IT'S TWICE AS HARD TO GIVE IT UP AND GET BACK TO YOUR OWN WORK.

SPEAKING OF WORK-- I SHOULD PROBABLY GET BACK TO WHAT I WAS DOING.

OKAY--LEARN THE HARD WAY. YOU'LL SEE WHEN YOU GET OLDER.

"THAT WEEKEND"

WELL I'M SORRY TRISH BUT I JUST DON'T HAVE TIME TO SEE YOU THIS WEEKEND. I'VE GOT TOO MUCH WORK TO DO. -----YEAH, WELL YOU SHOULD'VE THOUGHT OF THAT LAST WEEKEND WHEN YOU WERE TOO BUSY TO SEE ME.

ALRIGHT. BYE.

WHAT'S GOOD FOR THE GOOSE IS GOOD FOR THE GANDER-- WHATEVER THAT MEANS.

49

NOT THAT IT'S ANY OF YOUR BUSINESS--BUT NO, I HAVEN'T KISSED HIM. WE'RE JUST GOOD FRIENDS AT THIS POINT. WE HAVE FUN TOGETHER AND HE MAKES ME FEEL GOOD ABOUT MYSELF--SOMETHING YOU NEVER DID. THAT'S WHY I BROKE UP WITH YOU.

HEY, TAKE IT EASY! I WAS JUST ASKING! NO BIG DEAL! HEH..

WELL I'M FREE TO DO AS I PLEASE NOW, SO DON'T ASK ME AGAIN. I'D HATE TO HAVE TO LIE TO YOU.

gulp

DAYS LATER..

HMMM--MAYBE PART OF THIS IS MY FAULT. MAYBE I HAVE BEEN A BIT OF AN ASSHOLE. IT'S CERTAINLY POSSIBLE.

--AND I'M SORRY I'VE BEEN SUCH A SHITTY BOYFRIEND, BUT I CAN CHANGE. JUST GIVE ME ANOTHER CHANCE, BABE. C'MON--THIS IS WHAT YOU WANTED, ISN'T IT? SAY YES.

≥ SIGH ≤ NO, JOE--IT'S TOO LATE NOW. IT'D JUST BE A STEP BACKWARDS. IT'S OVER. WE'RE HISTORY.

B-BUT WE BELONG TOGETHER! YOU'VE SAID SO YOURSELF! YOU--YOU--YOU---

LOOK, THIS ISN'T EASY FOR ME EITHER-- BUT I HAVEN'T FELT THIS GOOD ABOUT MYSELF IN YEARS. PLUS I'M SEEING MORE OF GRAHAM NOW. I'M SORRY, BUT IT'S JUST TIME TO MOVE ON.

FINE! MOVE ON THEN! WHO NEEDS YOU?! IT'S YOUR LOSS NOT MINE!

SLAM!

AREN'T YOU EVEN **WORRIED** ABOUT THIS GUY TRISH'S BEEN SEEING?

NAH--I KNOW HER TOO WELL. SHE WON'T RUSH INTO ANYTHING. SHE'S JUST TRYING TO MAKE ME JEALOUS.

DON'T BE SO SURE. PEOPLE CAN SURPRISE YOU, Y'KNOW.

OH YEAH? WELL MAYBE **I'LL** SURPRISE **HER** BY GETTING A NEW GIRLFRIEND SOON! AND THIS TIME I'M GONNA BE MORE CHOOSEY. NO MORE **FROG-BODIES** FOR ME! I WANT ABSOLUTE PERFECTION.

BOY, TALK ABOUT SHALLOW. THAT ATTITUDE'S GOING TO DOOM YOU TO A LIFE OF PURE **FRUSTRATION.** YOU'VE GOT TO LEARN TO BE SATISFIED WITH WHAT YOU'VE GOT. QUIT *LOOKING* FOR GREENER PASTURES.

S-SO YOU THINK I M-MADE A MISTAKE LETTING TRISH GO?

LET'S PUT IT THIS WAY--- WHAT OTHER GIRL IN HER RIGHT MIND WOULD GO OUT WITH A GUY LIKE YOU? ESPECIALLY AFTER READING YOUR COMICS AND SEEING WHAT A CREEP YOU REALLY ARE?

OH GOD! YOU'RE RIGHT! I'VE PAINTED MYSELF INTO A CORNER! I'LL NEVER FIND ANOTHER GIRL LIKE TRISH!

WHAT AM I GONNA DO? I DON'T WANNA BE A BACHELOR THE REST OF MY LIFE!

CALM DOWN. YOU'LL MEET SOMEONE.

OH YEAH? WHEN? WHERE? HOW?

JUST GO UP AND START TALKING TO THEM.

I CAN'T DO THAT! I-I'M TOO SHY! I--

YOU CAN IF YOU WANT TO.

BUT I DON'T WANT TO!

THEN GET USED TO BEING A BACHELOR.

BUT I DON'T WANNA BE A BACHELOR!

WHOOOOA!!

EVENTUALLY..

...AND WHEN TRISH CALLS, I WANT YOU TO SAY I'M OUT WITH SOME GIRL AND THAT'LL MAKE HER JEALOUS, SEE? THAT WAY I CAN--

I DON'T KNOW JOE--

--I QUESTION YOUR MOTIVATION FOR EVEN **WANTING** TRISH BACK. FROM THE LITTLE I'VE SEEN OF YOU TWO TOGETHER, IT'S OBVIOUS YOU HAVE ABSOLUTELY **NO RESPECT** FOR HER. I'VE ONLY SEEN YOU CRITICIZE, BELITTLE AND DISCOURAGE HER.

NO! YOU'RE WRONG! I TRY TO HELP HER! I'VE BEEN CARTOONING LONGER THAN HER! I'M QUALIFIED TO--TO--

I'M MORE INCLINED TO THINK IT'S <u>YOUR OWN</u> **INSECURITY** AND FEELINGS OF **INADEQUACY** THAT MADE YOU HURT HER.

OH GOD--**YOU'RE RIGHT!** DEEP DOWN I CAN FEEL IT. OH--WHAT HAVE I DONE?

REGARDLESS--LIES AND DECEPTION ARE NO ANSWER. HONESTY'S ALWAYS THE BEST POLICY.

I KNOW I KNOW!! GOD, WHAT'S HAPPENED TO ME?!

YOU'RE JUST A VICTIM OF A SOCIETY THAT CONSPIRES TOWARDS YOUR UNHAPPINESS. EVERY DAY OUR MEDIA PROMOTES THESE UNATTAINABLE IDEALS OF THE OPPOSITE SEX THAT ONLY CAUSE INSECURITY, FRUSTRATION AND DISSATISFACTION AMONG SPOUSES.

AAAUGH!!

FINALLY..

P-PLEASE--YOU'VE G-GOTTA TAKE ME BACK! I DIDN'T KNOW WHAT I WAS DOING! I C-CAN CHANGE--I SWEAR! P-P-PLEASE--D-DON'T D-DO THIS TO ME! I N-NEED YOU!

I CAN'T BELIEVE HOW PERFECTLY OUR BODIES FIT TOGETHER! IT'S ALMOST LIKE WE WERE MADE FOR EACH OTHER!

MY THOUGHTS EXACTLY, TRISH.

HERE, HAVE A SEAT. I WANNA TELL YOU SOMETHING.

WHOA-- EASY.

N-NOW I KNOW THIS IS G-GONNA SOUND CRAZY--ESPECIALLY SINCE I'VE ONLY KNOWN YOU A FEW DAYS--BUT I-I HONESTLY THINK I-I LOVE YOU--AND--WELL--UH--

C'MERE

DID I EMBARRASS YOU? I CAME ON TOO HEAVY, DIDN'T I? I CAN--

PART THREE

FINALLY. HERE COMES "THE PEST" NOW.

HI GUYS. SORRY I'M LATE. I WAS ON THE PHONE WITH TRISH AND--

WHAT? YOU CALLED HER? BUT JUST YESTERDAY YOU SWORE YOU'D NEVER CALL HER AGAIN.

≥SIGH≥ I KNOW BUT I CAN'T HELP IT! I CAN'T STOP THINKING ABOUT HER. I KEEP HOPING SOMETHING'S CHANGED--THAT WE'LL GET BACK TOGETHER AGAIN. I STILL CAN'T BELIEVE ANY OF THIS IS HAPPENING...

TIME TO FACE REALITY, PAL..

--TRISH AIN'T COMING BACK. SHE'S BEEN SEEIN' THIS GUY GRAHAM FOR FOUR MONTHS NOW. SHE EVEN TOLD YOU SHE'S SLEEPING WITH HIM. FACE IT, SHE'S GONE. PUT HER BEHIND YOU.

I KNOW--YOU'RE RIGHT. I'M ALREADY SORRY I EVEN CALLED HER. I FEEL SO PATHETIC NOW. HER VOICE JUST UPSETS AND DEPRESSES ME.

I'VE JUST GOTTA BE FIRM AND STOP CALLING HER! IT'S THE ONLY WAY THESE WOUNDS ARE GONNA HEAL! I SWEAR, AS OF TODAY MY FINGERS WILL NEVER DIAL HER NUMBER AGAIN!

SOUNDS LIKE A GOOD IDEA TO ME.

OKAY--NOW LET'S GO EAT.

WAIT! FIRST WE'VE GOTTA GO TO THE BEGUILING! I'VE GOTTA SELL SOME OF THESE SHITTY COMICS! I'M BROKE!

≥GRUMBLE≥ ALRIGHT BUT MAKE IT QUICK.

HEH..HEH...I'M JUST FUCKIN' WITH YOU JOE. OKAY--LET'S SEE WHAT KIND OF SHIT YOU'RE TRYING TO UNLOAD THIS WEEK. HMMM... UH-HUH.. HMMM...CHRIST, YOU CAN'T EVEN PAY ME TO TAKE HALF OF THIS SHIT. JEEZ..

TAKE YOUR TIME. I'LL JUST LOOK AROUND THE STORE A BIT.

UH--ER--EXCUSE ME BUT I COULDN'T HELP OVERHEARING --- ARE YOU **REALLY** JOE MATT? THE GUY THAT DOES _PEEPSHOW_?

YEP! THAT'S ME-- I'M JOE MATT. DO I KNOW YOU?

GOD I'M LIKE YOUR BIGGEST FAN! THIS IS TOO FUCKIN' COOL! I CAN'T BELIEVE I'M STANDING HERE TALKING TO YOU! I FEEL LIKE I ALREADY KNOW YOU!

HEH..HEH.. I HEAR THAT A LOT.

ANYWAY MISTER MATT, MY NAME'S ANDY AND I PLAY BASS IN A LOCAL BAND HERE IN TORONTO CALLED THE STRING HOPPERS--

PLEASE-- CALL ME JOE. HEY! LET'S SEE WHAT BOOKS YOU BOUGHT THERE.

HMMM-- I DUNNO-- THIS GUY'S TASTE LOOKS PRETTY QUESTIONABLE...

ANDY, CAN WE GO NOW? I'M STARVING.

IN A MINUTE KIM.

THIS IS JOE MATT! HE DOES THAT COMIC BOOK _PEEPSHOW_ I WAS TRYING TO GET YOU TO READ THE OTHER NIGHT. REMEMBER? IT WAS THAT "IPANEMA" STORY WHERE HE GIVES HIS GIRLFRIEND A BLACK EYE.

OMIGOD! WOTTA DOLL!

?

DID HE JUST SAY BLACK EYE ?!

OH YEAH--

--WHY DID YOU GIVE YOUR GIRLFRIEND A BLACK EYE?

DON'T ASK HIM STUFF LIKE THAT! YOU'RE GONNA EMBARRASS HIM!

A-ACTUALLY SHE DID MOST OF THE HITTING IN OUR RELATIONSHIP! I WAS JUST KINDA GETTING EVEN I THINK-- I DUNNO--- HEH..HEH..

GOD I WISH I WAS DEAD.

WELL HURRY UP ANDY. I'LL BE OUTSIDE.

YOUR--UH-- GIRLFRIEND I ASSUME?

YEAH, THAT'S KIM.

ANYWAY JOE--NICE MEETING YOU. MAYBE SOMEDAY IF YOU'RE NOT TOO BUSY YOU'LL LET ME TAKE YOU OUT FOR DINNER OR SOMETHING. I KNOW HOW CHEAP YOU ARE.

GEE THANKS BUT--UH-- DON'T GET YOUR HOPES UP. I'M A PRETTY BUSY GUY Y'KNOW. HEH..HEH..

MAN, DID YOU GET A LOOK AT THAT GUY'S GIRLFRIEND? SHE WAS GORGEOUS! IT'S NOT FAIR I TELLYA..

Y'SHOULDA JUST FLASHED HER THAT ALLEGED HORSE-COCK YOU'RE ALWAYS BRAGGIN' ABOUT. SHE'D OF COME RUNNIN'.

HEH..HEH.. YEAH, RIGHT.

SHE HAD KIND OF A BIG BUTT BUT I COULD LIVE WITH IT.

EXCUSE ME MISTER--HOW MUCH IS THIS COMIC BOOK GOING TO BE WORTH IN A YEAR?

WHAT DO I LOOK LIKE? A **PRICE-GUIDE**?! GET THE HELL OUTTA HERE!

GODDAMN FUCKIN' KIDS. ANYWAY HERE'S YOUR MONEY.

FIVE BUCKS?! IS THAT ALL?? I PAID AT LEAST--

QUIT YOUR FUCKIN' WHINING OR YOU WON'T EVEN GET THIS.

AT LEAST I HAD A FAN COME UP TO ME. LET THAT BE A LESSON TO YOU GUYS -- WORK HARD AND MAYBE SOMEDAY YOU'LL HAVE FANS OF YOUR OWN.

GROAN

HEY LOOK! SEE THAT FANCY, FRENCH RESTAURANT OVER THERE? THAT'S WHERE TRISH AND I ATE THE VERY FIRST NIGHT WE EVER VISITED TORONTO. WE WERE SO EXCITED THAT NIGHT THAT MONEY WAS NO OBJECT. LITTLE DID I REALIZE BACK THEN THAT SOMEDAY I WOULD ACTUALLY END UP LIVING HERE.

IF ONLY SOMEONE COULD HAVE WARNED US.

THAT WAS OVER TWO YEARS AGO AND I CAN STILL REMEMBER THE MEAL--SHRIMP SOUFFLÉ AND CHEESE FONDUE. MMMMM-- IT WAS DELICIOUS. THE BILL CAME TO $42.50 AND I ACTUALLY TIPPED $7.00.

SOUNDS TRAUMATIC. NO WONDER HE NEVER FORGOT IT.

SIGH

WE WERE SO IN LOVE THEN.

COME ON JOE -- KEEP MOVING. DON'T LOOK BACK.

BUT I GOTTA CALL HER! IF I DON'T SHE'S LIABLE TO FORGET WHO I AM! AND IN THE MEANTIME THIS GRAHAM IS SCORING ALL KINDS OF POINTS WITH HER! I'LL SOON BE OUT OF THE RUNNING!

I GOT NEWS FOR YOU PAL-- YOU'VE BEEN OUT OF THE RUNNING FOR MONTHS NOW. SHE AIN'T COMING BACK.

B-B-BUT--

HOW MANY TIMES DO I HAVE TO TELLYA?! WAKE UP AND SMELL THE COFFEE! QUIT WAITING AROUND FOR A HAPPY ENDING!

BUT I DON'T KNOW WHAT TO DO! I CAN'T LIVE WITHOUT HER!

WHAT YOU NEED IS A DISTRACTION. Y'GOTTA MEET SOMEONE NEW TO TAKE YOUR MIND OFF OF TRISH. THAT'S HOW SHE GOT OVER YOU.

SETH, THIS IS **ME** WE'RE TALKING ABOUT, REMEMBER?! I NEVER MEET ANY GIRLS! AND EVEN IF I DID, I COMPLETELY LACK THE CONFIDENCE AND AGGRESSION NECESSARY TO--

DON'T START.

DON'T CALL HER--YOU'LL BE SORRY!
DON'T CALL HER--YOU'LL BE SORRY!
DON'T CALL HER--YOU'LL BE SORRY!
DON'T CALL HER--YOU'LL BE SORRY!
DON'T CALL HER--YOU'LL BE SORRY!
DON'T CALL HER--YOU'LL BE SORRY!

I CAN'T TAKE IT ANYMORE! I'VE GOTTA GET OUTTA HERE! SETH WAS RIGHT-- I'VE GOTTA FIND SOMEONE NEW! IT'S THE ONLY WAY! I'VE NOTHING TO LOSE!

I GUESS I'LL GO TO A NIGHTCLUB OR SOMETHING--EVEN THOUGH I HATE THOSE PLACES. STUPID TRENDY PEOPLE--LOUD, SHITTY MUSIC-- OVERPRICED BEER--SMOKE EVERYWHERE--

OH GOD, PLEASE DON'T LET ME REGRET THIS TOO MUCH!

ADMISSION $7.00

≤ GROAN ≤ WHAT AM I DOING HERE?! I CAN'T JUST APPROACH A TOTAL STRANGER! CHRIST, LOOK AT THIS GIRL--WHAT A GODDESS! I FEEL LIKE A GODDAMN DOG IN HEAT! SHE'S OUT OF MY LEAGUE ANYWAY--MAYBE IF I WAS YOUNGER OR HAD MORE HAIR. OH GOD, I HATE MYSELF...

HEY! JOE MATT! FAR OUT! WHAT'RE YOU DOING HERE?

YOU PROBABLY DON'T REMEMBER ME-- WE MET LAST WEEK IN THE BEGUILING COMIC SHOP! MY BOYFRIEND, ANDY, IS A BIG FAN OF YOUR WORK!

OF COURSE I REMEMBER YOU! UH-- BETH, WASN'T IT?

NO! KIM!

RIGHT! KIM!

YOU SEEM A BIT--UH-- DIFFERENT THAN WHEN WE FIRST MET. HEH..

I JUST READ ALL OF YOUR COMICS THE OTHER DAY! I LOVED THEM! BOY, YOU'RE REALLY ONE FUCKED-UP DUDE! HAHA!

HEH HEH

WELL THIS IS WHERE WE LIVE. WANNA COME IN FOR A MINUTE AND SAY HI TO ANDY?

SURE, WHAT THE HELL.

♪ AAAANDY --- GUESS WHO I FOUND-- ♪

HEY ANDY. HEH..

JOE MATT! COOL!

FIVE YEARS, HUH? THAT'S EVEN LONGER THAN TRISH AND I WENT OUT. HOW DO YOU GUYS DO IT?

KIM'S JUST THE RIGHT GIRL FOR ME. I'D MARRY HER TOMORROW IF SHE'D LET ME. RIGHT BABE?

YEAH..YEAH.. BUT WHAT'S THE HURRY? WE'RE STILL YOUNG.

THE TRICK IS TO ALWAYS KEEP WORKING AT IT. IT'S TOO EASY TO SLIP INTO COMPLACENCY AND START TAKING THE OTHER PERSON FOR GRANTED. JUST REMEMBER: THE GRASS IS ALWAYS GOING TO BE GREENER NO MATTER WHAT.

Y'GOT THAT RIGHT--

-- BUT HOW DO YOU STOP THAT FEELING OF INDIFFERENCE ONCE IT STARTS? IT SEEMS LIKE FAMILIARITY ONLY BREEDS CONTEMPT IN THE LONG RUN. IT GOT TO THE POINT WHERE I COULDN'T EVEN STAND THE WAY TRISH CHEWED HER FOOD.

I DON'T UNDERSTAND IT. HOW CAN LOVE JUST FADE LIKE THAT?

I DUNNO...

AWWW..

AND NOW TRISH IS WITH THIS NEW GUY?

≷ SIGH ≷ YEAH. IT TOOK HER ABOUT TWO SECONDS TO REPLACE ME TOO. SHE EVEN SAYS SHE'S HAPPIER WITH HIM NOW THAN SHE EVER WAS WITH ME.

CHEER UP! WE JUST HAVE TO FIX YOU UP WITH A NEW GIRL AND YOU'LL BE FINE. JUST LEAVE IT TO ME--I'M IN A BAND FOR CHRISSAKE.

REALLY?! YOU'D DO THAT FOR ME?!

JUST TELL ME WHAT YOU LIKE.

OBOY! THIS IS GREAT! HMMMM---LESSEE NOW-- FIRST OF ALL SHE'S GOTTA BE SKINNY. THAT'S REAL IMPORTANT. AND PREFERABLY WITH DARK HAIR. I GO FOR A BOHEMIAN, ARTISTIC TYPE AND I FIND ETHNIC GIRLS PARTICULARLY ENTICING. ASIAN, INDIAN, BLACK, GREEK---I DON'T CARE. BUT DON'T GET ME WRONG--WHITE GIRLS ARE FINE TOO, AS LONG AS THEY'RE SMALLER THAN ME, BUT NOT TOO SMALL. AND I PREFER SMALL BREASTS AND A FIRM BUTT. BIG EYES AND FULL LIPS ARE ALWAYS A BONUS TOO. AND HER CALVES AND THIGHS SHOULD BE THIN. AND SHE HAS TO BE A FAST WALKER AND NON-SMOKER AND BLAH BLAH BLAH---

OKAY--WELL--UH-- I'LL--UH--SEE WHAT I CAN DO.

I KNOW IT SOUNDS LIKE I'M ORDERING A PIZZA OR SOMETHING, BUT HE ASKED Y'KNOW. HEH--HEH--

THAT'S OKAY. I DON'T MIND.

HEY JOE, WHAT ABOUT KIM? IS SHE YOUR TYPE? WOULD YOU GO OUT WITH HER IF I WASN'T?

WELL--GEE-- HEH--HEH--I DUNNO-- PROBABLY--

OH ANDY, STOP IT.

UH--ANYWAY, I SHOULD PROBABLY GET GOING.

WELL THANKS FOR STOPPING BY, MAN. CALL ME SOMETIME AND WE'LL GET TOGETHER AND DO SOMETHING. OKAY?

YEAH, SURE.

AAAHH--THAT KIM. WHAT A CUTIE. SOME GUYS HAVE ALL THE LUCK.

--I'M TELLIN'YA SETH, HE'D BETTER FIND A GIRL FOR ME, OTHERWISE I JUST MAY BE TEMPTED TO STEAL HIS GIRLFRIEND. HAHA! YEAH, YEAH-- I KNOW BUT YOU SHOULD SEE HER. SHE'S PERFECT FOR ME. OF COURSE SHE'D HAFTA QUIT SMOKING--

SO ANDY--ABOUT THAT GIRL YOU SAID YOU'D FIX ME UP WITH? HAVE YOU--UH--

I'M WORKING ON IT BUT I DON'T KNOW--YOU'RE SO DARN FUSSY, IT MAY TAKE A WHILE.

THAT'S OKAY. I CAN WAIT.

AAAHHH--TEENAGE GIRLS! NOTHING LIKE 'EM, EH JOE?

TELL ME ABOUT IT. BUT AREN'T YOU MADLY IN LOVE WITH KIM?

SURE BUT I'M ONLY HUMAN Y'KNOW.

UH-HUH

HERE, LET ME PAY FOR THAT BOOK. I KNOW HOW BROKE YOU ARE.

BUT YOU JUST PAID FOR LUNCH AND POOL.

PLEASE, I INSIST.

WELL IF YOU INSIST--

--ACTUALLY, IF YOU'RE THAT ANXIOUS TO MEET A GIRL, YOU SHOULD JUST COME TO OUR GIG TONIGHT. THERE'S BOUND TO BE A TON OF BABES THERE.

HMMM--THAT'S NOT A BAD IDEA..

I'M CERTAINLY NOT GONNA MEET ANYONE BY SITTING AT HOME. WHO KNOWS? TONIGHT COULD BE THE BIG NIGHT. IT'S POSSIBLE...

I JUST WANTED TO MAKE SURE THERE WERE NO HARD FEELINGS ABOUT LAST SATURDAY NIGHT. I DIDN'T EVEN KNOW ANDY HAD A GIRLFRIEND. BUT I SWEAR, ALL WE DID WAS MAKE OUT A LITTLE. IT WAS NO BIG DEAL. WE WERE BOTH DRUNK ANYWAY. DON'T WORRY, IT WON'T HAPPEN AGAIN.

OKAY-- THANKS--

SO HOW'S THE BABE ACTION? HAVING ANY LUCK?

NAH.

DAYS LATER..

BUT I THOUGHT YOU KNEW BETTER THAN TO FOOL AROUND. WHY'D YOU DO IT?

≥ SIGH ≤ I DUNNO. I JUST CAN'T HELP MYSELF WHEN I GET DRUNK. IT WAS A DUMB THING TO DO.

I CAN'T BELIEVE I'M HEARING THIS! YOU SEEMED SO SENSIBLE. I THOUGHT YOU WANTED TO MARRY KIM. WHAT IF SHE DUMPS YOU NOW?

SHE WON'T. I'M JUST LUCKY KIM'S SO UNDERSTANDING. WE DIDN'T EVEN HAVE MUCH OF A FIGHT THIS TIME.

THIS TIME?! THERE WERE OTHERS?

A FEW.

WELL I THINK YOU'RE CRAZY. YOU DON'T KNOW WHAT YOU HAVE UNTIL YOU LOSE IT.

C'MON--A LITTLE KISSING'S NO BIG DEAL. KIM EVEN MADE OUT WITH AN OLD BOYFRIEND A FEW MONTHS AGO.

REALLY?

HELL, SHE'D PROBABLY EVEN KISS YOU. SHE REALLY LIKES YOU, Y'KNOW.

SHE DOES?!

BOY, IT SOUNDS LIKE THIS DOPE IS REALLY BLOWING IT. WHO KNOWS? PLAY YOUR CARDS RIGHT AND MAYBE YOU WILL GET HIS GIRLFRIEND.

YEAH AND DON'T FORGET HE SAID SHE LIKES ME ENOUGH TO KISS ME! HE SHOULD KNOW.

RRRING!

HELLO? TRISH?! UH--HI. YEAH, FINE. UH-HUH. WELL I DON'T MISS YOU. --UH-HUH--YEAH, OF COURSE I'VE BEEN AVOIDING YOU. I MEAN, WHAT'S THE POINT? WHY BOTHER? YOU DON'T WANT ME BACK.

WELL WHAT'S THE POINT IN THAT? ALL THAT MEANS IS WE'RE NO LONGER HAVING SEX THEN. AND THAT'S STUPID SINCE THE SEX WAS THE ONLY GOOD THING IN OUR RELATIONSHIP. BESIDES, I'VE GOT TOO MANY FRIENDS AS IT IS. YEAH? WELL IF YOU STILL LOVE ME THEN WHY DON'T YOU WANT ME BACK? YEAH--YEAH--I KNOW--

--BUT I NEVER WANTED TO BREAK UP! I JUST WANTED MORE SPACE. I DID NOT! I WAS TOTALLY COMMITTED TO YOU. YOU'RE THE ONE THAT WAS ALWAYS BREAKING UP WITH ME. OH SHUT UP--DON'T START THAT AGAIN. YOU'RE THE ONE THAT HAS A PROBLEM WITH PORN, NOT ME.

RESPECT **?!** HOW <u>COULD</u> I RESPECT YOU **?!** YOU HAD NO AMBITION AND YOUR TASTE IN EVERYTHING SUCKED **!** **WHAT ?!** YOU'RE CRAZY **!** YOU'RE THE ONE THAT WAS ALWAYS TRYING TO CHANGE ME **!** ALL YOU EVER DID WAS INHIBIT MY WORK AND FIGHT WITH ME **!** I'M GLAD YOU'RE OUT OF MY LIFE **!** Y'HEAR ME **?!** WHY DON'T YOU GO FUCK YOUR GODDAMN NEW

≷ CLICK ≷

C'MON, HAVE A FEW MORE. I MADE THESE SHRIMPS ESPECIALLY FOR YOU, JOE. I KNOW FROM YOUR COMICS HOW MUCH YOU LOVE SEAFOOD.

NO, REALLY--I COULDN'T EAT ANOTHER BITE. WELL MAYBE ONE MORE--

SO HOW'S MY DATING SERVICE GOING **?** HAVE YOU FOUND THE GIRL OF MY DREAMS FOR ME YET **?** HEH..HEH..

STILL LOOKING. ALTHOUGH I DO HAVE ONE POSSIBILITY..

OH YEAH **?!** WHAT'S HER NAME **?** HOW OLD IS SHE **?** WHAT'S SHE LOOK LIKE **?** IS SHE CUTE **?**

HER NAME'S MARY-- SHE'S AN OLD GIRL- FRIEND OF MINE. I THINK YOU'D LIKE HER. SHE'S GOT A GREAT PERSONALITY.

UH-HUH---AND--UH--JUST HOW OLD IS THIS MARY **?**

ONLY A FEW YEARS OLDER THAN YOU.

UH-HUH--I SEE. HMMM--AND--UH-- JUST HOW MUCH DOES THIS MARY PERSON WEIGH **?**

AND HOW TALL IS SHE **?**

WHAT COLOR'S HER HAIR **?**

SHE IS SKINNY, ISN'T SHE **?** CUZ IF SHE ISN'T--

HAHAHA! HE'S NOT EVEN SURE! HA!

C'MON--WHICH SIDE WON?! TELL US! NORTH OR SOUTH?

ALRIGHT--THAT'S ENOUGH!

HAHAHA! HEY JOE-- WHO WON THE FIRST WORLD WAR?

HAHAHA!

YOU CAN'T EXPECT ME TO REMEMBER EVERYTHING FROM HIGH SCHOOL. BESIDES, I'VE ALWAYS HATED HISTORY.

WHY'RE YOU GUYS PICKING ON JOE SO MUCH? I THOUGHT YOU WERE HIS FRIENDS. YOU SHOULDN'T RIDICULE HIM--DEEP DOWN WE'RE ALL BROTHERS.

AAHH--JOE KNOWS WE'RE JUST FOOLING WITH HIM. DON'T YOU JOE?

YEAH, TELL HIM JOE.

YEAH--IT'S OKAY ANDY, THEY'RE ONLY KIDDING. HEH IT DOESN'T BOTHER ME-- I'M USED TO IT. HEH..

THAT STILL DOESN'T MAKE IT RIGHT...

AWW... C'MON... JOE KNOWS DEEP DOWN WE REALLY LOVE HIM--DON'T YOU JOE?

H-HEY! STOP IT GUYS! PEOPLE ARE GONNA THINK WE'RE GAY!

TEE HEE!

--WELL, HOW COULD SHE _NOT_ FEEL SORRY FOR ME, THE WAY YOU GUYS WERE PICKING ON ME! HAHA! REALLY? NO WAY! EVEN IF SHE DID PREFER ME OVER ANDY, I'M NOT ABOUT TO MAKE A MOVE ON HER. SHE'D HAVE TO BREAK UP WITH HIM FIRST. NO! IT'S THE PRINCIPLE OF THE THING. STOP IT--HE'S A NICE GUY. HAHA! "JOE AND KIM" DOES HAVE A NICE RING..

DAYS LATER..

601

THE BEGUILING

HEY JOE -- WHERE'S THE SKIPPER?

SKIPPER?

?

Y'KNOW -- THE SKIPPER! THAT BALD-HEADED GOON THAT COMES IN EVERY FRIDAY. HE'S THE SKIPPER AND JOE'S GILLIGAN, HIS LI'L BUDDY. THEY'RE BEST PALS NOW SINCE SKIP BECAME JOE'S PERSONAL BODYGUARD. DEEP DOWN THEY'RE LIKE BROTHERS.

I WONDER WHO YOU'VE BEEN TALKING TO?

I ALSO HEAR Y'WANNA SLIP HIS WOMAN THE OL' SALAM. I'M SURE SKIP WON'T MIND -- AFTER ALL, WHAT'RE FRIENDS FOR? RIGHT? HAHA!

HAHA!

HE'LL PROBABLY EVEN LICK YOUR ASS CLEAN WHILE YOU'RE POKIN' HER!!

GRUNT PANT PANT GRUNT PANT PANT GR GRUNT PANT PANT

PANT PANT

OOOOHH.. THAT'S IT -- DON'T STOP! DON'T STOP!

77

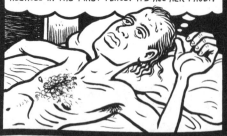

YOU'RE THINKING I HAVE A BIG BUTT, AREN'T YOU? I DON'T CARE--I KNOW I'M NOT YOUR IDEAL TYPE.

NONSENSE. IT'S A FINE BUTT.

C'MON--YOU DON'T REALLY EAT YOUR SCABS LIKE YOU SAY IN YOUR COMICS, DO YOU?

HEH..HEH.. 'FRAID SO.

WELL, HERE IT IS--MY FABULOUS ROOM! HEH..

WOW.

IT'S SO SMALL AND COZY---LIKE A CHILD'S ROOM. HEY, A FRANKENSTEIN STATUE! COOL..

UH-OH!

HEY! WHERE DID YOU GO?

UH--JUST A SEC!

THAT DOES IT-- FROM NOW ON I'M PEEING IN THE BATHROOM!

AN HOUR LATER..

WOW--YOU'RE RIGHT-- THESE VIEW-MASTER REELS ARE GORGEOUS!

SEE? WHAT'D I TELLYA? HUH?

PART
FOUR

MORNING, JAMES. MMMM...QUITE A SELECTION TODAY.

YES, SIR. I GATHERED THEM FROM THE EXOTIC WING OF THE MANSION.

OBOY! LET'S SEE...I'LL TAKE YOU.. ..AND YOU...AND YOU...AND YOU... AND YOU...AND YOU...AND YOU..

..AND OF COURSE, THE TWINS. HEH..HEH..

OKAY, GIRLS--LET'S ALL GO HIT THE HOT-TUB BEFORE ADJOURNING TO THE MASTER BEDROOM!

JAMES--FETCH SOME CHAMPAGNE AND LOBSTER TAILS.

RIGHT AWAY, SIR.

MMMMM...THE WATER'S PERFECT.. ..NICE AND WARM.. HURRY UP, JOE!

MMMMMM...CAN'T WE JUST GO STRAIGHT TO THE BEDROOM? PLEASE?

PATIENCE, GIRLS. HEY, WHAT'S THAT RINGING SOUND?

RRRING!

REALLY? IN THE MALL? WINDOW DISPLAYS, HUH? WOW..THAT'S SO WEIRD. Y'KNOW, I HAVEN'T EVEN SEEN HER SINCE COLLEGE, AND THAT WAS LIKE SEVEN YEARS AGO. PLUS I QUIT WRITING TO HER AFTER SHE GOT MARRIED. I COULDN'T HELP IT-- I WAS OBSESSED WITH HER FOR YEARS ...

..PROBABLY CUZ I LOST MY VIRGINITY TO HER. THAT'LL DO IT, Y'KNOW. PLUS SHE WAS AN ABSOLUTE KNOCK OUT. I CAN STILL REMEMBER THIS LITTLE, BLACK TANK-TOP SHE HAD ...AAAAAHH...THE WAY IT COMPLEMENTED THAT DARK MANE OF HAIR SHE HAD AND SHOWED OFF THOSE GOLDEN RIBS AND FLAT STOMACH....AAAAAHH...MEMORIES..¿ AHEM¿ SO..UH...DID YOU TALK TO HER AT ALL? REALLY? DOES SHE HAVE ANY CHILDREN? I'LL BET SHE--

DIVORCED?! REALLY?!!

AND SHE ASKED FOR MY PHONE NUMBER? UH-HUH.. ..UH-HUH.....WOW! THIS IS INCREDIBLE..

OBOY! I CAN'T WAIT! YOU DID SAY NO CHILDREN, RIGHT? HAHA JUST CHECKING. OKAY MONICA... THANKS FOR CALLING. SAY HI TO EVERYONE FOR ME. BYE.

AAAAAHH... LAURA...LAURA... WHO'D OF THOUGHT? IT MUST BE FATE...

JOE! COME BACK! WHAT ABOUT US?!

HEY! WHO'S THE NEW GIRL WITH THE TANK-TOP?

JOE, WHY IN GOD'S NAME ARE YOU WASHING THEIR WINDOWS, HUH?

OH, HI CHARLES.

I MADE AN ARRANGEMENT WITH ANNA WHERE I'D DO A FEW ODD JOBS AROUND THE HOUSE EVERY MONTH IN EXCHANGE FOR A REDUCTION IN MY RENT.

HAHAHA! ALWAYS LOOKING TO SAVE A BUCK, AREN'T YOU? YOU REMIND ME OF A GUY I ONCE KNEW WHO--

CHARLES! ≥GRUNT≥ I HOPE YOU HAVE THE THREE MONTHS RENT YOU OWE ME.

≥GULP≥ UH...SORRY ANNA... NOT YET. I'M UH...STILL WAITING FOR A CHECK FROM SOMEONE.

WELL THEN -- GET A JOB! THIS ISN'T A CHARITY HOUSE WE'RE RUNNING, Y'KNOW.

YOU'LL GET YOUR MONEY.

≥GRUNT≥ Y'MIGHT AS WELL KNOCK OFF, JOE. THOSE WINDOWS LOOK FINE.

YES MA'AM.

BRUNO! I'M STARTING THE VIDEO!

93

--THAT'S RIGHT, OPERATOR... AND HER FIRST NAME'S LAURA. REALLY?! HOLD ON--I'LL GET A PENCIL...

FOUR RINGS... MAYBE SHE'S NOT HOME. I SHOULD JUST HANG UP NOW BEFORE SHE--

☀! H-HI..LAURA? IT'S JOE MATT! YEAH! HEH..HEH...THAT'S RIGHT...YEAH, SHE TOLD ME. HEH. THIS IS REALLY WEIRD, ISN'T IT? HEH..SO...UH..HOW'S IT GOING? LONG TIME NO SEE! HEH..HEH...YEAH, SEVEN YEARS. HEH..HEH..

3 HOURS LATER..

--YEAH, SO WRITE ME AND ENCLOSE A PICTURE OF YOURSELF AND THEN I'LL DO THE SAME. HEH..HEH...YEAH, RIGHT. WE'LL SEE. OKAY,...TALK TO YOU LATER.

♫ BYE BYE..♫

--AND IT WENT GREAT! WE TALKED FOR HOURS! YOU SHOULDA HEARD ME--I WAS TOTALLY FLIRTATOUS! I FIGURED, WHAT THE HELL-- SHE'S ALL THE WAY DOWN IN THE SUBURBS OF PHILADELPHIA--WHAT'S SHE GONNA DO? HAHA! AND SHE ATE IT UP! SHE WAS EVEN WORSE THAN ME! SHE MAY EVEN COME UP TO VISIT!

GREAT.

SO THIS LAURA WAS YOUR ORIGINAL "OBJECT OF DESIRE," HUH?

YUP. HEY, SPEAKING OF OBJECTS OF DESIRE--GET A LOAD OF THAT GIRL BEHIND THE COUNTER. AYE CARUMBA!

DAYS LATER...

THANKS A LOT FOR DINNER, GUYS. SORRY TO EAT AND RUN LIKE THIS, BUT MY SHIFT STARTS AT SIX. NICE MEETING YOU, JOE.

ADIOS.

BYE MARY.

LIKEWISE.

SO? WHAT DID YOU THINK OF MARY? NICE, HUH?

SURE. SHE WAS REAL NICE.

YEAH, AND SHE LIKED YOU TOO! I COULD TELL.

YEAH?

YEAH! SO ASK HER OUT! I'LL GIVE YOU HER PHONE NUMBER!

NO..NO... I DON'T THINK SO. SHE WAS CUTE AND EVERYTHING BUT Y'KNOW -- RED HAIR AND FRECKLES AREN'T MY TYPE.

BESIDES, I'VE ALREADY GOT SOMETHING IN THE WORKS.

AWWW...ARE YOU SURE? C'MON...YOU TWO WOULD MAKE SUCH A CUTE COUPLE.

AT LEAST GIVE HER A CHANCE. IF YOU WANT, I COULD..

QUIT PUSHING HIM! HE ALREADY SAID HE'S NOT INTERESTED! ARE YOU DEAF?

WHAT? I'M JUST TRYING TO HELP HIM!

?

HEH... YEAH, KIM -- IT'S NOT ANDY'S FAULT. I'M JUST AN INGRATE. HEH..HEH..

YEAH, RIGHT. NOTHING'S EVER HIS FAULT. I'M JUST ACTING IRRATIONAL, I SUPPOSE. LIKE ALWAYS.

A WEEK LATER...

OH, HI BRUNO. I JUST WANTED TO RETURN YOUR VCR AND THANK YOU FOR LETTING ME :::UH.. ?

HEY BRUNO...YOU OKAY? YOU LOOK A LITTLE--

W-WHAT AM I DOING? I-I C-CAN'T SEEM TO--TO--TO--

H-HERE...SIT DOWN. THAT'S IT. J-JUST TAKE IT EASY.

W-WHO AM I? WHAT AM I DOING? I-I-I DON'T--

BRUNO! WHAT ARE YOU DOING OUT HERE? I TOLD YOU TO STAY PUT! THE AMBULANCE IS ON IT'S WAY!

I-I CAN'T UNDERSTAND M-MY--I-I--

?

JOE, STAY WITH HIM! I'M GONNA WAIT OUTSIDE FOR THE AMBULANCE.

B-B-BUT ANNA! I-I-I-I

W-WHERE AM I DOING? I-I--

OW! !

W-W-WHA... OW!
I-I-I-D-D-DON'T
OW! W-WHA?

J-J-JUST TAKE IT EASY, BRUNO...UH.. HELP'S ON THE WAY.. ...EVERYTHING'S GONNA BE ALRIGHT...HEH..

--AND THEN THEY CARRIED HIM OUT ON A STRETCHER. IT WAS THE STRANGEST THING...I COULDN'T FIGURE OUT WHAT WAS HAPPENING TO HIM. HE JUST KEPT HOLDING HIS HEAD AND GOING, "OW! OW! OW!"

WELL, IT'S OBVIOUS WHAT WAS HAPPENING...

.. HE WAS HAVING A STROKE. POOR GUY. BUT WHAT DID HE EXPECT FROM A LIFETIME OF SMOKING AND EATING JUNK IN FRONT OF THE TV? I JUST HOPE HE DOESN'T DIE. ANNA WOULD EITHER GO INSANE OR KILL HERSELF.

A STROKE? REALLY?

SURE. EVERY TIME HE SAID "OW!", ANOTHER BLOOD VESSEL IN HIS BRAIN WAS EITHER CLOGGING OR BURSTING. EVEN IF HE LIVES, HE'LL DEFINITELY SUFFER SOME BRAIN DAMAGE. TO WHAT EXTENT I..

UGH...BURSTING BLOOD VESSELS...OOHH.. ..EXCUSE ME...I'VE GOTTA LIE DOWN...

A WEEK LATER...

?? BUGS? WHERE DID THEY COME FROM? IT COULDN'T HAVE BEEN THE BEANS...THEY MUST'VE BEEN IN THE RICE.

WELL THERE'S NO WAY I'M THROWING OUT THIS MUCH FOOD OVER A FEW LITTLE BUGS. I CAN JUST FISH 'EM OUT...

≥ GRUNT ≥ HERE, JOE-- Y'GOT SOME MAIL.

OH, THANKS ANNA. SO WHAT'S THE WORD ON BRUNO? IS HE COMING HOME SOON?

NOT FOR A FEW WEEKS. THEY WANNA KEEP HIM IN SPEECH THERAPY UNTIL HE IMPROVES A BIT.

HEY, HAVE YOU SEEN CHARLES AROUND LATELY?

UH..NO..

MMMMMMMM...WHAT SMELLS SO GOOD?

OH, IT'S JUST BEANS AND RICE WITH TOMATO PASTE. I MAKE IT A LOT.

MMMMM...YOU DON'T MIND IF I TASTE IT, DO YOU?

UH..ACTUALLY... ..I..UH..UH..

MMMMMM

101

102

OH, C'MON--HOW CAN YOU BE SO CYNICAL WHEN YOUR AURA'S SO POSITIVE? YOU SHOULD AT LEAST GIVE IT A CHANCE. YOU'D BE SURPRISED--IT REALLY WORKS. EVERYTHING'S PREDESTINED, Y'KNOW.

≷ GROAN ≷ PLEASE.. ..STOP...SAVE IT FOR SOME- ONE ELSE...

YOU'RE A VIRGO, AREN'T YOU? I CAN TELL!

YES..YES...IT'S ALL TRUE..I'M A VIRGO.

HAH! I KNEW IT! WHAT TIME WERE YOU BORN?

STOP IT... PLEASE... I BEG OF YOU...

EXCUSE ME--I'M LOOKING FOR SOME LITERATURE ON ASTRAL PROJECTION..

BACK THERE--NEXT TO REINCARNATION.

WHERE?

BACK THERE! NO--NO-- TO YOUR LEFT! OVER A BIT. A LITTLE MORE... NOW LOOK STRAIGHT UP.

UH..KIM? I THINK I'D BETTER BE GOING. I'VE GOT SOME...UH.. SHOPPING TO DO. HEH..

THANKS FOR DROPPING BY! I'LL CALL YOU! MAYBE WE CAN GET TOGETHER AND DO SOMETHING SOMETIME.

UH..SURE...THAT'D BE GREAT. ANYTIME. UH..SEE Y'LATER.

≷ YEESH ≷ THANK GOD I NEVER MADE A MOVE ON HER THAT NIGHT...

GRRRR....WHY DON'T THEY LEAVE? ARE THEY WAITING TO SEE THE BATHROOM? COULD THAT BE IT? **WAIT!** WAS THAT A GIRL'S VOICE I JUST HEARD? DAMN! I CAN'T BE SURE...

FUCK IT-- I'M NOT SPENDING THE REST OF MY LIFE IN THE GODDAMN BATHROOM! CHANCES ARE IT'S JUST SOME GUY LOOKING AT ROOMS. AND EVEN IF IT IS A GIRL, SHE'S PROBABLY UGLY.

!

--AND THIS IS JOE. HIS ROOM'S RIGHT NEXT TO THE KITCHEN. JOE, THIS IS JILL.

HELLO.

JILL'S AN EXCHANGE STUDENT FROM CHINA. SHE'S OVER HERE STUDYING ANTHROPOLOGY.

OH REALLY? HOW NICE! AH-HEH...

ACTUALLY, I'M CONCENTRATING ON ANCIENT ASSYRIA.

W-WELL..NICE M-MEETING YOU..HEH.. I-I'M GOING INTO MY ROOM NOW... HEH...HERE I GO...HEH...BYE!

BUMP!

C'MON, I'LL SHOW YOU THE BATHROOM.

NICE MEETING YOU TOO.

KOFF KOFF KOFF **KOFF**

OH GOD--**HOW MORTIFYING!!** BUT PLEASE LET HER MOVE IN! I'LL DO ANYTHING! **PLEASE!** PLEASE PLEASE PLEASE PLEASE PLEASE!

PART FIVE

RRRRING!

≥ GROAN ≤ H-HELLO? OH..HI SETH. NO..
IT'S OKAY... I WAS JUST..UH..RESTING.
≥ KOFF KOFF ≤ YEAH..THAT'S RIGHT. HUH?
WHAT'S NEW? UH..WELL..

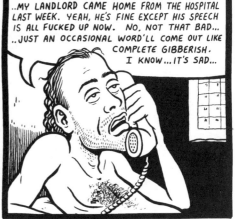

..MY LANDLORD CAME HOME FROM THE HOSPITAL
LAST WEEK. YEAH, HE'S FINE EXCEPT HIS SPEECH
IS ALL FUCKED UP NOW. NO, NOT THAT BAD...
..JUST AN OCCASIONAL WORD'LL COME OUT LIKE
COMPLETE GIBBERISH.
I KNOW...IT'S SAD...

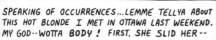

BZZZZ!

HI MARY. THANKS FOR COMING OVER.

HEY, NO PROBLEM. THANKS FOR INVITING ME OVER. HAHA.

WELL, I JUST FIGURED..IT'S ONLY FAIR THAT YOU SHOULD GET TO CHECK OUT MY SWANKY PAD TOO. HEH...

HEY, I'M PARKED IN YOUR DRIVEWAY. I HOPE IT'S OKAY..

OF COURSE IT'S OKAY.

WHOSE CAR IS THAT OUT THERE ?! THEY'RE GONNA HAFTA MOVE IT.. WE NEED THAT SPACE. ≳GRUNT≲

UH...IT'S HER CAR.. B-BUT...

I'LL GO MOVE IT.

SORRY ABOUT MY LANDLADY. I DON'T KNOW WHAT HER PROBLEM IS.

IT'S OKAY.. REALLY.

MY ROOM'S JUST UP THESE STAIRS. FOLLOW ME.

O-OKAY.

C'MON....ARE YOU SURE YOU DON'T WANT SOME OF MY COMICS? IT'D BE A GOOD WAY TO GET TO KNOW ME REAL QUICK.

NO..NO...I TOLD YOU, I'D RATHER GET TO KNOW YOU IN PERSON.

SUIT YOURSELF.

LATER..

--AND THIS IS MY COLLECTION OF PEE-WEE'S PLAYHOUSE CARDS. THIS THIRD FINGER/NOSE CARD IS ULTRA-RARE, BUT I FINALLY GOT IT.

HEY, I'VE GOT A FEW OF THESE..BUT I HAD NO IDEA THERE WERE SO MANY...

WOOOOW.....YOU EVEN HAVE PEE-WEE VIEW-MASTERS! HAHA..I JUST LOVE PTERRI..."I AM NOT A BABY, PEE-WEE!" HAHAHA!

HMMM...I'M GETTING DÉJA-VU..

UH...HOW 'BOUT A GAME OF CHESS?

SURE, I LOVE CHESS. ARE YOU ANY GOOD?

HEH..HEH...DON'T WORRY...I'LL GO EASY ON YOU.

SOON..

DAMN...I DIDN'T EVEN SEE THAT COMING. SHIT... THAT WAS MY QUEEN TOO..

JOE! JOE!

HEY, THAT'S MY LANDLADY!

JOE! COME QUICK! HURRY! HURRY!

SHE'S OUTSIDE. I WONDER WHAT'S WRONG?

HEY, HEY -- I UNDERSTAND! I'M PROBABLY NOT READY FOR ANYTHING EITHER! HEH... I MEAN, WE BARELY EVEN KNOW EACH OTHER! WHADDAYA SAY WE JUST FORGET THE WHOLE THING? OKAY?

YEAH.. THAT SOUNDS LIKE A GOOD IDEA.

I-IT DOES?

OKAY...SO...UH.. YOU'LL CALL ME SOMETIME? HEH..

YEAH.. I'LL CALL YOU.

--AND BASICALLY I JUST WANTED TO APOLOGIZE FOR LUNGING AT YOU LIKE THAT. I COULDN'T HELP IT -- I'VE ALWAYS BEEN ATTRACTED TO INDEPENDENT, SKINNY GIRLS LIKE YOURSELF. HEH..HEH...

? WHAT? REALLY? I'M NOT? WELL WHAT KIND OF GUYS ARE YOU ATTRACTED TO? MUSICIANS?! OH, C'MON... YOU CAN'T BE SERIOUS -- DON'T TELL ME YOU'RE ONE OF THOSE! UH-HUH..YEAH.. ..YEAH... I KNOW BUT-- ...YEAH ....YEAH... WELL, I GUESS I CAN SORTA UNDERSTAND IT...

..HEH... Y'KNOW, IT'S IRONIC BECAUSE YOU'RE NOT EXACTLY MY TYPE EITHER. HAHA! NO, REALLY-- I SWEAR. IF YOU EVER READ MY COMICS, YOU'LL SEE I DON'T USUALLY GO FOR REDHEADS. I WAS MAKING AN EXCEPTION FOR YOU. HAHA! YEAH, WELL...YOU SHOULD BE FLATTERED.

YEAH, BUT DON'T YOU SEE? LIFE DOESN'T WORK THAT WAY. YOU CAN'T GO AROUND WITH A PRECONCEIVED LIST OF QUALIFICATIONS. LIFE'S TOO SHORT. YOU HAVE TO JUST LET THINGS HAPPEN. I MEAN, DON'T YOU THINK IT'S HARD ENOUGH JUST FINDING SOMEONE COMPATIBLE?

BESIDES, WHAT'S THE BIG DEAL WITH MUSICIANS ANYWAY? HELL, MOST OF THEM AREN'T EVEN ARTISTS--THEY JUST WANNA BE STUPID ROCK STARS ON MTV. THOSE DOPES ARE A DIME-A-DOZEN. ON THE OTHER HAND, JUST TRY FINDING A GOOD CARTOONIST. HEH..HEH...THAT'S RIGHT...

AN HOUR LATER..

--FAIR ENOUGH. THAT'S ALL I'M ASKING FOR--JUST A CHANCE. OKAY, MARY... SATURDAY NIGHT IT IS.

ADIOS, MY DEAR. HEH.. HEH..

--AND I THINK SHE'S JUST AFRAID OF RELATIONSHIPS IN GENERAL. Y'KNOW, SHE HASN'T BEEN IN ONE FOR YEARS, SO I'VE GOTTA PROCEED VERY CAUTIOUSLY. PATIENCE AND PERSEVERANCE--THAT'S MY MOTTO.

GOOD BOY. BUT DON'T PLAY IT TOO COOL--SOMETIMES Y'GOTTA STRIKE WHILE THE IRON'S HOT.

SOON..

--WELL, IF YOU HATE WAITRESSING SO MUCH, WHY NOT DO SOMETHING ELSE? SOMETHING YOU ENJOY?

I DUNNO...IT'S JUST NOT THAT EASY FOR ME. I ENJOY SO MANY THINGS BUT I COULD NEVER--

135

136

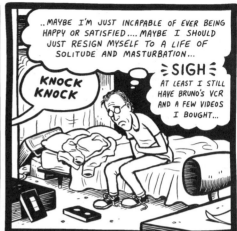

PART
SIX

--AND THEN WE WALKED HOME IN TOTAL SILENCE. ≶SIGH≶ IT WAS JUST AWFUL.

SOUNDS LIKE YOU TWO DON'T HAVE MUCH IN COMMON.

MAYBE YOU SHOULD JUST FORGET ABOUT HER.

FORGET ABOUT HER ?! ARE YOU CRAZY ? THIS IS MY BIG CHANCE !

AN OPPORTUNITY LIKE THIS ONLY COMES ALONG ONCE IN A LIFETIME. I'M JUST WAITING FOR THE RIGHT TIME AND PLACE TO MAKE MY MOVE.

BUT YOU BARELY KNOW HER. YOU DON'T EVEN SOUND LIKE YOU LIKE HER VERY MUCH.

OH, I LIKE HER ALRIGHT. SHE'S PERFECTION ! SHE'S GOT A FACE LIKE AN ANGEL ....SKIN AS SMOOTH AS PORCELAIN .... BEAUTIFUL BROWN EYES ... AND ALL OF THAT LUSH SILKY BLACK HAIR JUST CASCADING DOWN... OOOHHHH... I LOVE IT...

WELL, AT LEAST SHE'S BETTER THAN C.W.

OH CHRIST ! THAT REMINDS ME -- C.W.'s BEEN CALLING ME ALL WEEK ! HE'S COMING INTO TOWN SOON AND HE KEEPS BUGGING ME TO MEET HIM FOR LUNCH...

JUST TELL HIM YOU'RE BUSY !

I DO, BUT HE KEEPS CALLING BACK. AND HE SOUNDS SO DESPERATE AND LONELY. I FEEL BAD FOR HIM. I MEAN, HE'S LIVING IN A TENT FOR CHRISSAKES. ≶GROAN≶ AND HE'S CALLING FROM A PAY-PHONE OUT ON A HIGHWAY SOMEWHERE...

DON'T DO IT. YOU'LL BE SORRY. TRUST ME.

I KNOW...I KNOW..

WELL, I DO THIS COMIC BOOK CALLED _PEEPSHOW_, SEE ? IT'S AUTOBIOGRAPHICAL, ALTHOUGH I DON'T LIKE TO CALL IT THAT.

OH, MAY I SEE ONE ?

NO NO NO ! THEY'RE WAY TOO PERSONAL ! THEY'RE MORE FOR COMPLETE STRANGERS ! HEH..HEH..

B-BESIDES IT'S NOT EVEN REALLY M-ME ! I-IT'S MORE LIKE AN EXAGERRATED C-CARICATURE ! HEH..HEH..HEH..

C'MON, JUST SHOW ME A LITTLE...

WELL...OKAY...BUT JUST ONE PAGE....**OOPS !** DON'T LOOK AT THIS PANEL. OKAY... NOW, THIS IS ME ....AND THIS IS MY OLD GIRLFRIEND, TRISH. SHE DUMPED ME FOR ANOTHER GUY.

HOW AWFUL.

WELL, TO TELL THE TRUTH... I WASN'T EXACTLY THE WORLD'S GREATEST BOYFRIEND. BUT I LEARNED A LOT FROM THE EXPERIENCE AND I PLAN TO BE MUCH MORE GIVING OF MYSELF WITH THE NEXT GIRL.

THAT'S NICE.

WELL, I'M SURE YOU'LL FIND SOMEONE SOON... AS LONG AS YOU'RE NOT TOO FUSSY.

ME ? FUSSY ? HEH...HEH.. ARE YOU KIDDING ?

THAT'S GOOD.

I'M THE EXACT OPPOSITE -- I'M REAL FUSSY. I WANT SOMEONE LIKE THIS HISTORY PROFESSOR I HAD LAST YEAR. HE WAS AMAZING. HE KNEW ABSOLUTELY EVERYTHING ABOUT ASSYRIAN CULTURE. PLUS HE WAS TOTALLY OUTGOING AND ATHLETIC. AND HE EVEN DROVE A PORSCHE ! ≩SIGH≩ HE WAS PERFECTION ...

Y'DON'T SAY...

HEY... I LIKE THE WAY YOU'VE DONE UP YOUR ROOM.

THANKS. UH.. WOULD YOU LIKE TO COME IN?

Y'KNOW... RIGHT BEFORE YOU MOVED IN, I WASHED ALL THE WINDOWS IN HERE.

≟ YAWN ≟

HEY, WHAT'CHA READING HERE? HMMM... ANCIENT BABYLON, HUH? WHERE'S OL' HAMMURABI AND THAT CODE OF 282 LAWS THAT HE ISSUED BACK IN 1750 B.C.?

UH.. HE'S IN THERE..

AAAHHH... I SEE YOU LIKE CLASSICAL MUSIC. BEETHOVEN... MOZART...

YES, I FIND IT VERY CONDUCIVE TO STUDYING.

HMMM... I'LL BET IT'S REALLY RELAXING. I SHOULD TRY IT SOMETIME WHILE WORKING.

YOU'RE WELCOME TO BORROW A TAPE IF YOU'D LIKE.

THANKS.

BEETHOVEN

WELL, IF BEETHOVEN'S GOOD ENOUGH FOR SCHROEDER, HE'S GOOD ENOUGH FOR ME.

SCHROEDER? WHO'S HE?

NEVER MIND. WAIT HERE -- I'LL BE RIGHT BACK.

153

COOOO...
COOOO...

COO-COO YOURSELF.

--AND WHEN YOU LISTEN TO JONATHAN RICHMAN, PAY CLOSE ATTENTION TO HIS LYRICS. HE'S GOT A REAL, CHILDLIKE CHARM THAT I LOVE. NOW, WITH TOM WAITS, I RECOMMEND YOU START WITH _RAINDOGS_ AND THEN _SWORDFISH TROMBONES_. Y'KNOW, NOT MANY PEOPLE KNOW IT, BUT TOM--

I-I MAY NOT HAVE TIME TO--

OOPS! DROPPED ONE.

ELVIS COSTELLO

WHEW LUCKILY, THE CASE DIDN'T BREAK. SOMETIMES THEY CAN--

?

CHRIST-- HER CALVES ARE **HUGE!** THEY LOOK LIKE TWO, BIG, MILK-FED WATER BALLOONS! I--

UH.. I SHOULD PROBABLY GO TO BED SOON. I HAVE CLASSES TOMORROW.

S-SURE.

THE NEXT DAY..

HER CALVES ?! OH BROTHER! THIS IS SO TYPICAL OF YOU.

I KNOW... I KNOW.

I JUST HOPE TO GOD YOU NEVER RUN INTO MOTHER THERESA. I COULD JUST SEE YOU-- YOU'D START CRITICIZING HER IMMEDIATELY! YOU FIND FAULT WITH EVERYONE YOU MEET!

I CAN'T HELP IT -- I'M A VIRGO. WE'RE CRITICAL BY NATURE.

TEE HEE!

HEY, LOOK -- A SALE ON VCR'S! BOY, I COULD REALLY USE ONE.

A VCR?

ALL VCR'S **30% OFF**

DON'T YOU ALREADY HAVE ONE?

NAH...THAT WAS MY LANDLORD'S. I WAS JUST BORROWING IT.

≷ SIGH ≷ I REALLY MISS HAVING A VCR, BUT THEY'RE JUST SO DAMN EXPENSIVE.

I'LL BET YOU DON'T MISS THE VCR HALF AS MUCH AS THOSE "NATURE FILMS" YOU WERE ALWAYS RENTING! HAHA!

JOE MATT -- YOU'RE A FUCKIN' ASSHOLE!

!

155

LATER..

" DEAR JOE, HERE ARE YOUR TAPES BACK. SORRY, BUT I DIDN'T LIKE ANY OF THEM. THANKS ANYWAY. JILL "

BAH. I'LL BET SHE DIDN'T EVEN LISTEN TO THEM..

..AT LEAST I TRIED TO LISTEN TO HER LOUSY TAPE. IT'S NOT MY FAULT IT PUT ME TO SLEEP.

OH WELL... MAYBE SPARKY ATE SOME OF THAT TOFU I PUT IN HERE THIS MORNING.

♪ SPARKY... ♪

DAMN.

157

159

163

167